Dear Parent:

Congratulations! Your child i
the first steps on an exciting journey.
The destination? Independent reading!

STEP INTO READING® will help your child get there. The program offers five steps to reading success. Each step includes fun stories and colorful art. There are also Step into Reading Sticker Books, Step into Reading Math Readers, Step into Reading Phonics Readers, Step into Reading Write-In Readers, and Step into Reading Phonics Boxed Sets—a complete literacy program with something to interest every child.

Learning to Read, Step by Step!

Ready to Read   Preschool–Kindergarten
• big type and easy words • rhyme and rhythm • picture clues
For children who know the alphabet and are eager to begin reading.

Reading with Help   Preschool–Grade 1
• basic vocabulary • short sentences • simple stories
For children who recognize familiar words and sound out new words with help.

Reading on Your Own   Grades 1–3
• engaging characters • easy-to-follow plots • popular topics
For children who are ready to read on their own.

Reading Paragraphs   Grades 2–3
• challenging vocabulary • short paragraphs • exciting stories
For newly independent readers who read simple sentences with confidence.

Ready for Chapters   Grades 2–4
• chapters • longer paragraphs • full-color art
For children who want to take the plunge into chapter books but still like colorful pictures.

STEP INTO READING® is designed to give every child a successful reading experience. The grade levels are only guides. Children can progress through the steps at their own speed, developing confidence in their reading, no matter what their grade.

Remember, a lifetime love of reading starts with a single step!

For a great teacher, Mr. Ken May—M.M.-K.

BARBIE and associated trademarks and trade dress are owned by, and used under license from, Mattel, Inc.
Copyright © 2011 Mattel, Inc. All Rights Reserved.
Published in the United States by Random House Children's Books, a division of Random House, Inc., 1745 Broadway, New York, NY 10019, and in Canada by Random House of Canada Limited, Toronto.

Step into Reading, Random House, and the Random House colophon are registered trademarks of Random House, Inc.

Visit us on the Web!
StepIntoReading.com
www.randomhouse.com/kids
www.barbie.com

Educators and librarians, for a variety of teaching tools, visit us at
www.randomhouse.com/teachers

ISBN 978-0-375-86927-3 (trade) — ISBN 978-0-375-96927-0 (lib. bdg.)
Printed in the United States of America   10 9 8

Random House Children's Books support the First Amendment
and celebrates the right to read.

Barbie i can be...
A Teacher

By Mary Man-Kong

Illustrated by Kellee Riley

Random House 🏠 New York

Miss Jones is a teacher.

Barbie learns
to be a teacher,
too.

She helps
teach a class.

The class is happy
to see Barbie.
They show her
their schoolwork.

Anna shows Barbie
around the classroom.

Anna shows Barbie
the class pets.

Barbie helps feed
the cute bunnies
and the furry hamster.

Maggie gives the bunny
a carrot.

Maggie loves pets.

One day,
she can be
a pet vet.

Miss Jones makes a reading circle.

She reads a book
to the class.

The class writes
their own stories.
Barbie helps.

Emily writes
a princess story.

Emily loves
to write.
One day, she can
be an author.

The kids study sea animals.

Barbie makes animal art
with them.

Suzy paints a crab.

Suzy loves
sea animals.
One day, she can be
a marine biologist.

It is snack time!
Barbie helps
the class.
They make cupcakes!

Kate loves to bake.
One day,
she can be a chef.

Barbie teaches the kids about space.

She shows the class
pictures of stars
and planets.

Lisa finds pictures
of the planets.

Lisa loves space.
One day, she can be
an astronaut.

Anna likes
to help Barbie.

She likes
to help Miss Jones.
And she likes
to help other kids.

Anna has an idea.
One day, she can be
a teacher!

Barbie thinks Anna
will be a great
teacher.
Barbie can be
a teacher, too!